City of Gold

FIONA FRENCH

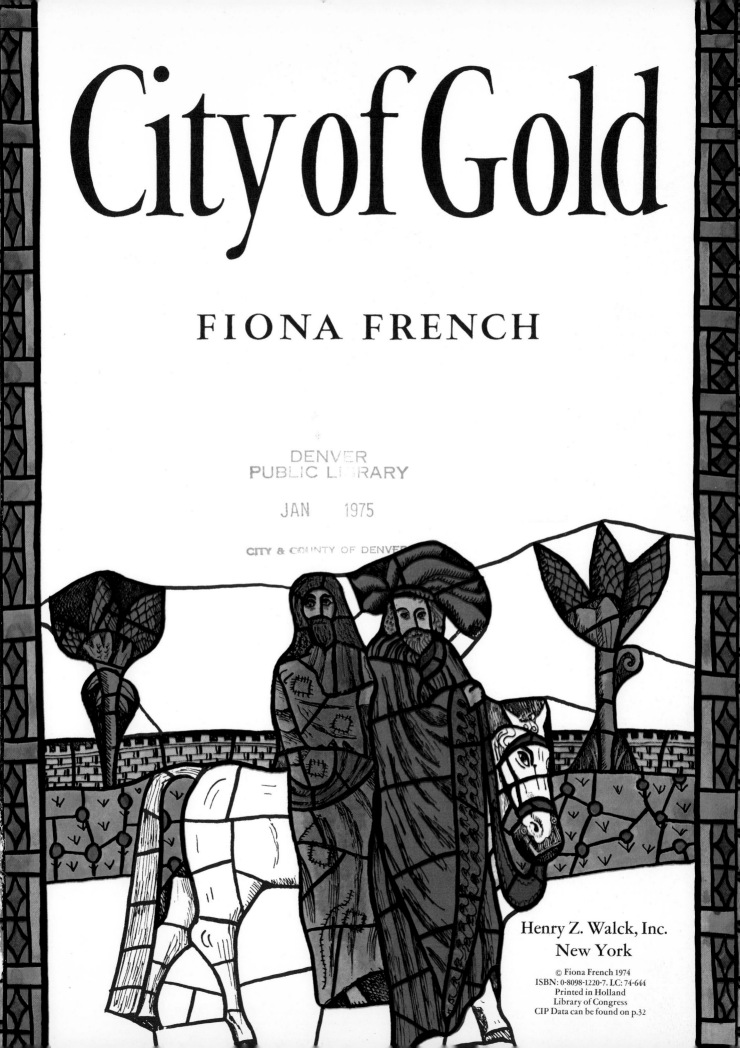

Henry Z. Walck, Inc.
New York

© Fiona French 1974
ISBN: 0-8098-1220-7. LC: 74-644
Printed in Holland
Library of Congress
CIP Data can be found on p.32

In olden days there was a City of Gold, with towers and domes that shone in the sun. But the people in the City were sorrowful because the town was plagued by a terrible Demon.

There were two roads leading to the City: one was wide and smooth, the other narrow and stony. The Demon sat at the end of the wide road and seized all the travellers who came along it. He took them down to his fiery kingdom, and all the people inside the City wept.

smooth high road

difficult road

brambles.

Not far away lived two brothers. John was hardworking and kind. He felt sorry for the people in the City and decided to go and fight the Demon.

Thomas his brother was merry and idle. He too had heard about the Demon. "I will go and conquer him," he said, "and the people will make me king. I shall be rich and powerful."

So they set out. At the crossroads stood two signs. One said "The City of Gold", and pointed to a steep, narrow road. The other said "Smooth road". John felt tempted to follow that road.

But then he remembered
the sad people in the City,
and took the narrow way.
Thomas chose the wide
road. "I expect this leads to
the City as well," he said.
"Anyway it is an easier road."

SMOOTH ROAD
LEADS TO
GOOD COMPANY AND
riches.

As he rode along,
Thomas met a
jolly nobleman, who
called out: "The City
of Gold is far away.
Stay at my castle awhile,
and we will hunt and
feast and dance. Make
life a holiday."

Thomas could not resist the
invitation. It was just the life
he enjoyed. He rode with his new
friend to his castle, and was the
most cheerful and clever of all
the guests.

Meanwhile, John
was toiling along
the narrow road.
It was a hard climb.
All at once a beggar
appeared, and pleaded
with John for food
and money.

John gave him all
the food in his bag
and all the money in
his purse. Then he
went on his way.

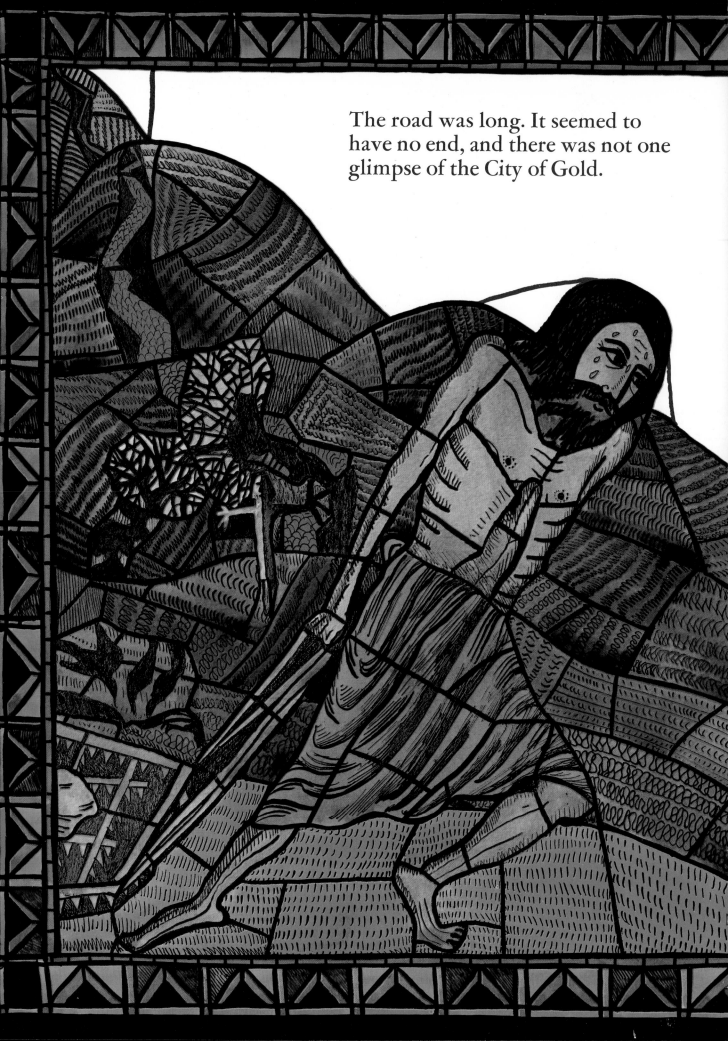

The road was long. It seemed to have no end, and there was not one glimpse of the City of Gold.

John had to work in the fields to earn his bread. At night he slept in the hay. Winter came, and still he searched for the City of Gold.

At last, Thomas grew tired of his
life of pleasure, and he thought
again of the City of Gold. He mounted

his horse, with all his treasure, and
sped along the smooth road.
But there at the end the Demon waited,
and Thomas trembled with fear. Then
he saw John walking along the narrow
path.

"He wears rags, and he's so thin, I can see his bones from here," thought Thomas. "But if I give him my rich cloak and some jewels

the Demon will mistake
him for me. Then
I shall be able to
get into the City."
So Thomas went to
meet his brother, and
wrapped him in his
own cloak, and hung
shining jewels round
his neck. Then he stood
back while John went
towards the gates.

Immediately, the Demon sprang upon him, and seized him in his strong arms. John fought bravely, but he was soon overcome. The Demon held John in a grip of iron, and flew straight into the mouth of his fiery pit.

Thomas rushed after them and saw his brother disappearing into the flames. "What have I done?" he cried. And he shouted in remorse: "Demon, you have the wrong man. I came along the smooth highway. It is I you should take." But the Demon laughed.

Thomas was full of grief, but now he used his wits. Quickly he collected all his treasure and bundled it up to look like a man.

He tied a rope round the neck and heaved the figure into the mouth of the burning cave.

"Demon, here I come," he cried, and
the bundle fell into the flames.
The Demon saw the new intruder,
heard the voice and seized the bundle
in his powerful arms. But in his haste,
he let go of John, who was thrown
out of the cave. Thomas grasped his
brother's hand, and ran with him
to the gates of the City.

The Demon was angry to not let go of the precious though that it dragged him fiery kingdom, and since he treasure the Demon was see him escape, but he would bundle. It was so heavy down to the depths of his would not let go of his never seen again.

John and Thomas were safely
inside the City of Gold. John
forgave his brother for the trick
he had played on him, for it was
after all Thomas's courage and
cleverness that had conquered the Demon.
And Thomas forgot that he had
ever wanted to be king.

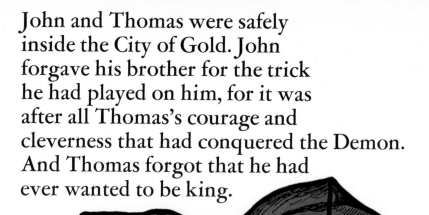

And the whole City
was happy to be free
at last of the Demon
at the gates.

Library of Congress Cataloging in Publication Data. French, Fiona. City of gold. SUMMARY: Two brothers set out on different roads to fight the Demon who guards the City of Gold   [1. Fairy tales]   I. Title.PZ8.F895Ci   (Fic)   74-644   ISBN 0-8098-1220-7